BUILDER MOUSE

Words and pictures by Sofia Eldarova

CLARION BOOKS • Houghton Mifflin Harcourt • Boston New York

Clarion Books
215 Park Avenue South
New York, New York 10003

Clarion Books is an imprint of Houghton Mifflin Harcourt Publishing Company.

www.hmhco.com

The illustrations in this book were done in
watercolor, pastel, and pencil on paper.
The text was set in 20 pt. McKenna Handletter NF

Library of Congress Cataloging-in-Publication Data is available.
LCCN: 2014043107

Manufactured in Malaysia
TWP 10 9 8 7 6 5 4 3 2 1
4500553714

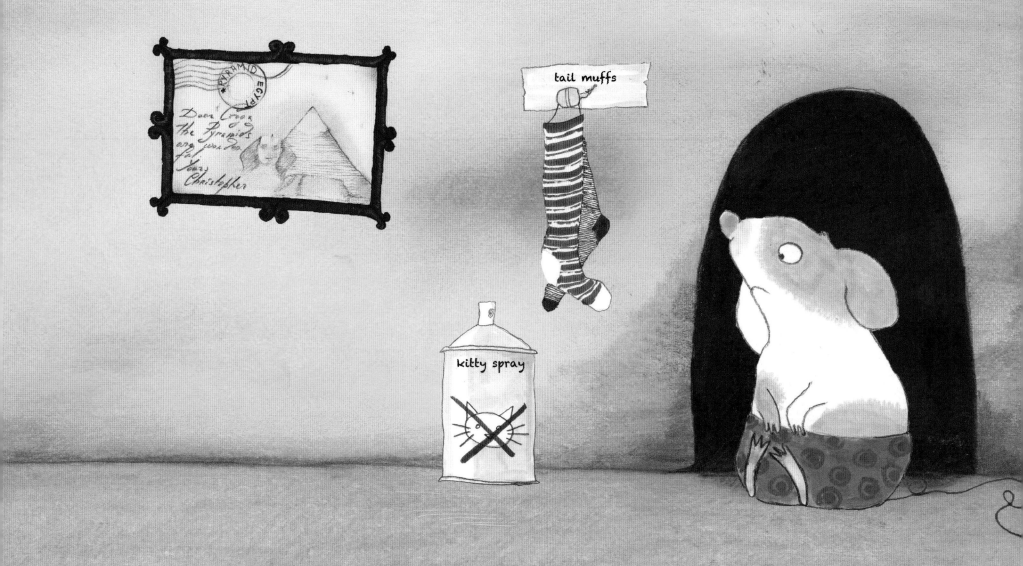

EDGAR loves to build. He especially likes
to build very tall things from leftovers he finds all
around. One day, he hopes to become an architect.

His best friend, Toby,
likes finding leftovers too.
His favorites are salami,
cheese, and chocolate cake.

But he is not a picky eater.
This makes life challenging.

On Monday, Edgar built an arch out of a melon slice and pretzel sticks. Toby loved the curve and thought the combination of salty and sweet was yummy.

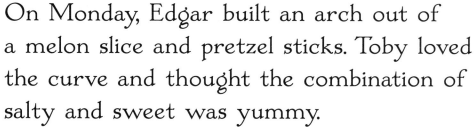

On Tuesday, Edgar made a tower out of apples and oranges. Toby admired it from every angle and found it crisp and refreshing.

On Wednesday, Edgar constructed a pyramid made entirely of beans. Toby thought this was Edgar's craftiest work ever and was delighted that it tasted just like chicken.

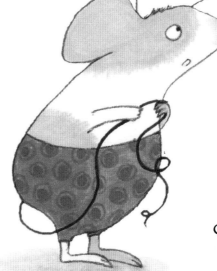

"What's for lunch?" asked Toby on Thursday.

"I am an architect, not a cook!" Edgar was fed up.
He packed his bag and left home to find someplace
where his talents would be appreciated.

Subway E D G A R

The subway looked perfect.

Edgar quickly built a castle
from peanuts, chips, and chocolate
bars. The subway mice found it
irresistibly tasty.

Café Edgar

"Perhaps I need to find someplace where the mice are less hungry," Edgar said. A restaurant seemed just the spot.

The restaurant mice did
appreciate his cheese dome,
but not in the way Edgar
had hoped.

"Delicious, mouthwatering, lip-smacking!" they shouted.

Next, Edgar spotted a museum. "Surely here,"
he said, "the mice will see beyond the food."

The arty mice were very curious about Edgar's candy mural. After studying it carefully for some time, they all agreed that it needed to be digested to be fully understood.

Edgar left the museum and shuffled slowly along the streets of the city, wondering if his work would ever be appreciated.

He was beginning to miss home and
his best friend. Although Toby was
always hungry, he understood Edgar's
work. Edgar wondered what leftovers
Toby had collected today and what
could be built from them.

Edgar walked and walked and walked, unsure where to head next, when suddenly he found himself near a very familiar brick wall.

And
a very
familiar
mouse hole.

Toby was overjoyed to see Edgar.
"I really missed you and your
wonderful, full-flavored towers!
You are a great architect, Edgar."

"Come on," said Edgar. "Let's see what leftovers
we can find—I feel like building a tasty castle!"

"I have a better
idea, Edgar."

"My own wooden building blocks!
Thank you, Toby!"

Edgar built a beautiful tower right away.

Toby thought it was stunning . . . .

. . . and, fortunately,
not the least bit tasty.

SHAPE OF THINGS TO COME

ARCHITECTURE EXHIBITION OF
EDGAR CAMEMBERT

Tale of a Tail Gallery • 8 Paw Road
October 28

the
ART
of
MODERN LIVING

ARCHITECTURE EXHIBITION OF
edgar camembert

Whiskers & Claws Gallery
12 Sheez Avenue
September 1 to 24